# Hansel and Gretel

### Retold by Kay Brown
### Illustrated by Gerry Embleton

**DERRYDALE**

A division of Crown Publishers, Inc.
New York

© Award Publications Ltd. MCMLXXVIII
Spring House, Spring Place
London NW5, England.

Library of Congress Catalog Card Number : LOC 79-84829

All rights reserved

This edition is published by Derrydale, a division
of Crown Publishers, Inc., One Park Avenue
New York, New York 10016

a b c d e f g h

Printed in Belgium.

Hansel and Gretel lived with their stepmother and their father, a poor woodcutter, in a tiny, tumbledown cottage on the edge of a forest. They had always been poor but, when our story starts, the woodcutter had had no work for weeks and there was not a scrap of food in the house.

One night, the children's stepmother persuaded her husband that the only thing he could do was to take the children deep into the forest and leave them there.

He was very upset by this idea as he loved his children dearly, but the stepmother was a hard and selfish woman and at last he agreed that, as there was no food for any of them, there was nothing else to be done. But because they were so hungry, Hansel and Gretel were unable to go to sleep and they overheard the plan. Gretel was very frightened, but Hansel bravely said "Don't worry little sister, I'll think of something."

Later that night, when his parents were asleep, Hansel put on his shabby coat, opened the door quietly and slipped out. In the moonlight, all the white pebbles in the garden shone brightly: Hansel filled his pockets with as many as they would hold, then crept back into the cottage. He tiptoed to Gretel's bed and whispered "Don't worry about tomorrow, I have a plan. Go to sleep now." Then he went silently to bed.

Next morning the woodcutter woke the children very early; he tried to be cheerful, saying "It's a fine day – let's go deep into the forest to cut wood" but his heart was very unhappy.

As the children followed him along the woodland path, however, Hansel dropped from his pockets the white stones he had collected the night before, one by one.

After many hours they reached a thick, cold part of the forest they had never seen before; the trees were very close and dark and Gretel was afraid. The woodcutter told the children to wait for him while he went to cut wood and, kissing them both gently, he left them together.

After a while the children could no longer hear the sound of his axe and realized they were lost and quite alone.

Gretel couldn't understand why her brother was cheerful and unafraid but, much later when darkness fell and the moon began to shine, Hansel showed her what he had planned.

There, shining in the moonlight, was one of the white pebbles he had dropped that morning . . . and beyond that, another and another . . . Gretel stopped crying and, hand in hand, the children followed the pebble path all night, back to their cottage.

Their father was delighted to see them safely back home again, and because he had managed to sell some of the wood he had cut, there was now a little food for them to share. But, after a few days, all the food that was left was half a stale loaf and the stepmother again persuaded her husband to take the children to the forest and leave them there.

Hansel had been expecting this and, from his hiding place by the door, heard all that was said. He was very sad, but decided to go out again when his parents were asleep to collect white pebbles as before. But oh dear! – the cunning stepmother had locked the door and taken the key. There was nothing Hansel could do but go to bed.

However, before they left next morning to go to the forest, the woodcutter gave his children a piece of bread each.

As they walked deeper into the wood, Hansel stopped from time to time to break off a few crumbs from his bread and drop them along the path. At last they reached the thickest, darkest part of the forest and, as before, the woodcutter left his children, having kissed them lovingly.

Gretel felt sure Hansel had another plan to take them safely home again, and they both waited until darkness fell and the moon's bright light shone through the tall branches. But when Hansel took Gretel's hand to lead her back the way they had come, he couldn't see the breadcrumbs he had scattered. Birds had eaten every crumb!

The children tried several paths, which seemed always to end in a thicker, darker part of the forest than they had left. For hours they wandered, feeling hungry and miserable, for they had shared Gretel's piece of bread long before.

When evening fell the next day they were exhausted. Hansel found a hollow log and they both crawled inside; with their arms tight around each other they were soon fast asleep. While they slept, the kind birds of the forest, who had been watching from the trees, flew down silently with leaves in their beaks and covered the children with a warm, leafy blanket.

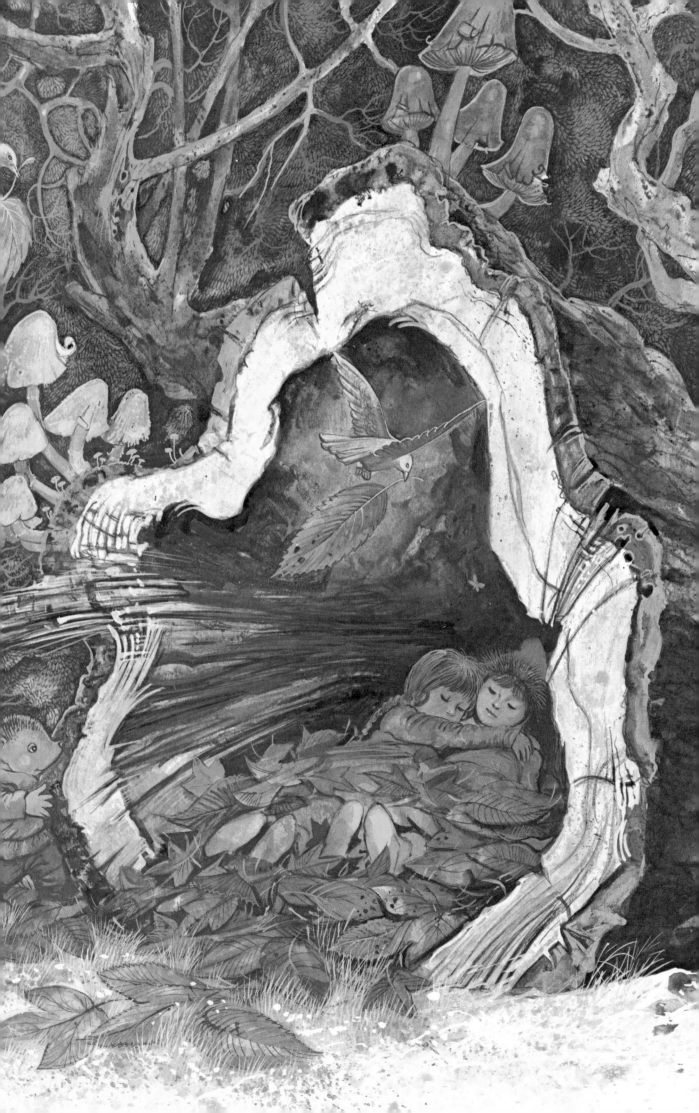

In the morning Hansel and Gretel were hungrier than ever. They were stiff and weak, but again began to walk hoping to find the way home. They wandered from path to path, across clearings and through brambles.

After a while Hansel realized they were not alone; a beautiful bird had been following them and now it sang to them from a low branch and fluttered its wings, as if saying "Follow me, follow me."

So they did and very soon they saw a shape through the trees. The bird went ahead of them and settled . . . on the roof of a marvellous cottage.

When Hansel and Gretel came closer, they saw that instead of stone, the walls were made of bread and cake, the roof of icing and the windows of clear sugar and everything was decorated with coloured sweets. The happy children ran to the house and hungrily broke off pieces to eat.

They were so hungry and excited they didn't notice someone shuffle out of the cottage! They both jumped when they heard a dry old voice say "Ah, dear little children, how young you are! – Come with me, come into my little house." Gretel was frightened but Hansel thought no-one bad could live in such a wonderful cottage, so they followed the bent old woman inside.

What Hansel and Gretel didn't know was
that the old woman was really a witch: she had
built the tasty cottage to attract children and,
when she had them safely inside, she would kill,
cook and eat them!

So, having Hansel and Gretel inside
the house, she kicked the door shut with a bang!
She seized Hansel by the wrist and dragged him
to a tiny wooden cage hanging from a beam.

Then she shut and locked the door, leaving Hansel screaming and kicking and Gretel crying miserably in a corner.

"Little boy, little boy, now you're locked in I can see your small legs all boney and thin" she cackled.

"So you'll eat by day and you'll eat by night, and in under a week you'll be plump alright."

Hansel shouted and Gretel cried, but it was no use. The horrid old woman made Gretel cook huge, fattening puddings for Hansel and watched him eat every scrap.

Each day the old witch would shuffle over to the cage and poke Hansel's leg with her sharp finger to feel how fat he was getting. However, the witch had very poor eyesight and wore extra strong glasses to help her see.

This gave Gretel an idea. She hid the witch's one pair of glasses then took Hansel a log from the firewood.

He tied the piece of wood
onto the end of his shoe and,
every time the old woman poked
him to see if he was ready for
the oven, Hansel made sure she
poked not his leg – but the stick!
In this way the children managed
to fool the old woman for several
weeks, but she began to grow
impatient.

One morning she suddenly said "Fat or thin, you shall be my lunch today, little boy!"

Gretel was heartbroken and cried as she worked all morning. The witch made her light the fire under the oven and fetch water to boil, while she prepared dough for the bread. When all was ready the witch called to Gretel.

"Creep into the oven, girl," she said. "If it's hot enough we'll bake the bread first."

But, because she was a cunning and wicked old witch, what she really meant to do was push Gretel inside the oven and enjoy <u>both</u> children for lunch! However, in the weeks Gretel had lived with the witch she had grown to mistrust her and now she guessed what was going to happen.

She said, in a little voice, "I don't know how to do it – How do I get in?"

"Stupid girl" said the witch. "There's a door big enough for two like you! I could even get in there myself!" and saying this the old woman put her head and shoulders into the oven. This was just as Gretel had hoped and, with a sharp push from behind, the witch was inside the oven and the door slammed fast behind her – bang! With the witch's howls echoing round the cottage Gretel snatched up her keys from the table and ran to Hansel.

"We're safe, we're safe!" she cried happily as she opened the cage. "The old witch is in the oven!" Hansel jumped down and hugged his sister – they danced around the cottage laughing and singing until they were quite dizzy!

Leaving the house – and the witch! –
the children ran out into the sunshine
hand in hand.

As they left the clearing several small
birds fluttered and hovered in front of
them: they seemed to be saying
"Follow us, follow us."

So, trustingly, Hansel and Gretel
followed the birds through the trees.
After several hours, and just as the sun
was setting, the birds flew away.

There, in the evening light, the
children saw a little house. They were
safely home!

Their father's sad face filled with joy when he opened the door. Hansel and Gretel told him all about the magic cottage, the wicked witch and how they had escaped. Then the woodcutter told his children that he had been very unhappy since he left them in the forest; their stepmother had died soon after and he had searched the woods every day for the children.

He had some good luck, however, a shopkeeper in the town had asked him to carve animals and figures to sell and now he had more orders than he could fill, so they would never again be poor and hungry.

Hansel and Gretel slept that night in their own beds and they and their father lived together for many, many years in great happiness.